BATHTIME WITH Rai

Story by Marcus Smith II
Illustrated by Tiara Boyd

METROPOLITAN LIBRARY SYSTEM
"SERVING OKLAHOMA COUNTY"

13TH & JOAN

For permission requests, write to the publisher, addressed "Attention: Permissions Coordinator," 205 N. Michigan Avenue, Suite #810, Chicago, IL 60601. 13th & Joan books may be purchased for educational, business or sales promotional use. For information, please email the Sales Department at sales@13thandjoan.com.

Illustrated by Tiara Boyd

Printed in the U. S. A.
First Printing, August 2020

Library of Congress Cataloging-in-Publication Data has been applied for.

Hardcover ISBN: 978-1-953156-09-9

You will never have another today with your child for tomorrow is sure to come and they will be a little older than they were today. Embrace the gift of today.

Meet Rai (Pronounced RY):

After a full day of fun at Granny's house, Mommy and Daddy are excited to take Rai home for even more special time together.

When they all arrive at home, Mommy and Daddy take Rai upstairs to begin their evening family activities.

Once up the stairs, Rai runs to the bathroom and points to the tub with excitement, reminding her parents of how much she loves bathtime! "Not just yet Rai, we've got a few more things to do with you," says Daddy!

While Daddy runs the water for her bath, Mommy takes Rai to her room to pick out a nice pair of pajamas.

And then he reads her favorite story!

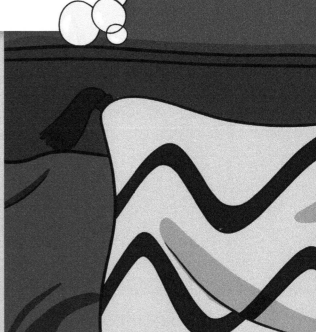

After story time, Rai runs over to the tub and plops her hand into the warm water. The bubbles look like clouds floating on the water.

"Alright Rai, looks like your water is ready," says Daddy.

While in the tub, Daddy sings Rai's favorite bath time song and drops in her toys one by one. The sound of laughter and love fill the whole room.

Mommy even bought Rai an alphabet book that she can play with in the tub.

Daddy washes Rai's hair and makes sure that she is nice and clean before bed.

The best part of bath time is snuggling into a warm towel and more laughter with daddy.

Now dry and ready for bed, Daddy teaches Rai to spell her name with the purple polka dot letters on the wall just before preparing to tuck her in.

Even though Daddy tries to put Rai to bed, she always asks him to read just one more book.

And every night, Rai falls asleep in Daddy's arms.

As he whispers, Sweet dreams Rai. Meet you at bath time again tomorrow.

Letter To Rai,

Dear Sarai,

I cherish each moment that I get to spend with you. I never take it for granted, and this is time you can't ever get back. Kobe, who was and remains one of my idols, was an awesome girl dad to his daughters Natalia, Gigi, Bianka and Capri. I want to display the same love and affection with you. This book shows our appreciation for you coming into this world. Bath time will forever be the staple for us bonding and creating memories that will last for a lifetime. We will be able to inspire other fathers and daughters to do the same. Psalms 37:4 says "Take delight in the Lord, and he will give you your heart's desires." Sarai, remember that you are a queen and success is not a destination but rather a mindset. Your mother and I will be there every step of the way to help you navigate your journey through the world. Your mother and I thank God every day for bringing you in to this world. We love you so much!

Sincerely,
Your Dad

CPSIA information can be obtained
at www.ICGtesting.com
Printed in the USA
LVHW071106220421
684629LV00038B/565